SABAN'S POWER RANGERS MEGAFORCE

ALIEN ATTACK!

By Ace Landers

SCHOLASTIC INC.

12 11 10 9 8 7 6 5 4 3   13 14 15 16 17 18/0
Printed in the U.S.A.   40
First printing, September 2013

Troy was in class, taking a pop quiz. But his mind kept drifting. He kept thinking about this morning's encounter. He had been alone in the woods, when he heard something behind him.

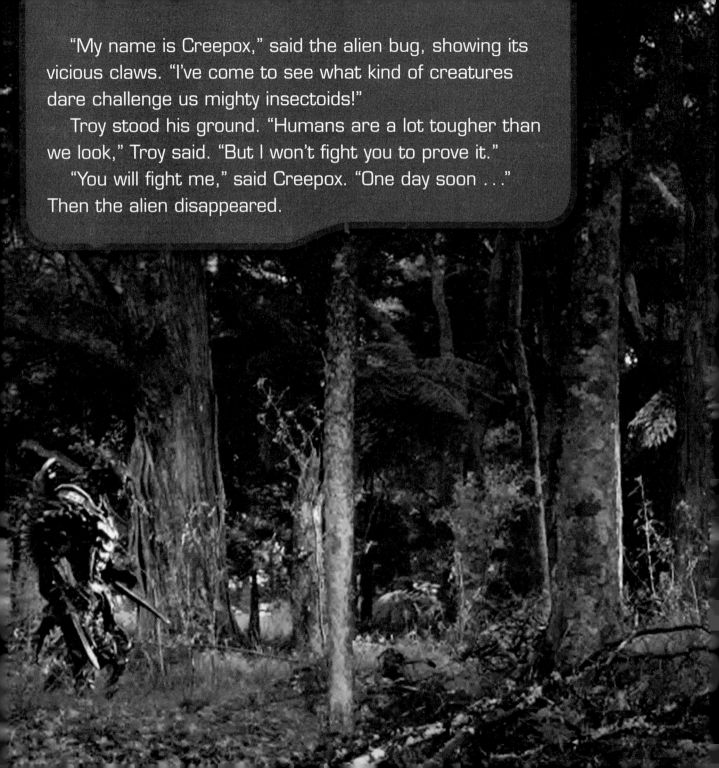

"My name is Creepox," said the alien bug, showing its vicious claws. "I've come to see what kind of creatures dare challenge us mighty insectoids!"

Troy stood his ground. "Humans are a lot tougher than we look," Troy said. "But I won't fight you to prove it."

"You will fight me," said Creepox. "One day soon . . ." Then the alien disappeared.

Later that day, Jake asked Gia if he could walk her home from school.

"Why?" joked Gia. "Are you afraid to walk by yourself?"

"No, I, um," Jake stuttered, "I just wanted to talk to you."

Deep in space, Creepox, Admiral Malkor, and Vrak made plans to destroy Earth.

Vrak wanted to study the humans and find their weaknesses, but Creepox believed that humans could be easily squashed by the bugs. Admiral Malkor agreed with Vrak and called upon the evil Yuffo to learn the best way to defeat humans.

Jake and Gia were walking when they saw flying saucers in the sky!

The two teens followed the saucers to find people were being abducted! Quickly, they morphed into the Black and Yellow Rangers.

But the saucers flew together to make one giant alien bug. "Mega Rangers! You're the perfect specimens for my research!"

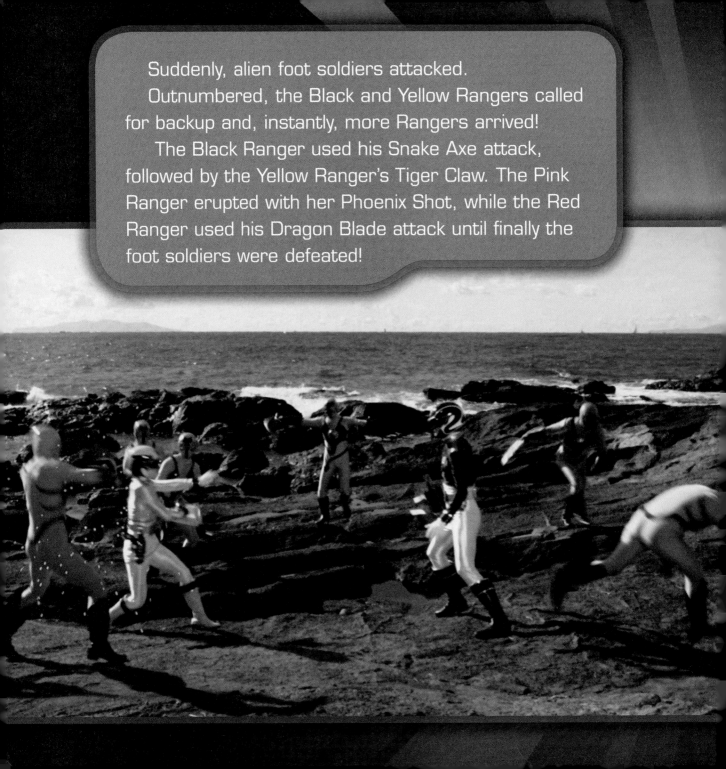

Suddenly, alien foot soldiers attacked.

Outnumbered, the Black and Yellow Rangers called for backup and, instantly, more Rangers arrived!

The Black Ranger used his Snake Axe attack, followed by the Yellow Ranger's Tiger Claw. The Pink Ranger erupted with her Phoenix Shot, while the Red Ranger used his Dragon Blade attack until finally the foot soldiers were defeated!

Yuffo launched a fleet of saucers at blistering speeds that hammered the Rangers.

Then Yuffo shot tiny blasts that exploded into a wall of fire around the Rangers.

"Incendiary attacks are extremely effective!" cackled Yuffo. "Destroying the human race will be child's play! Perhaps an electric shock will finish them off?"

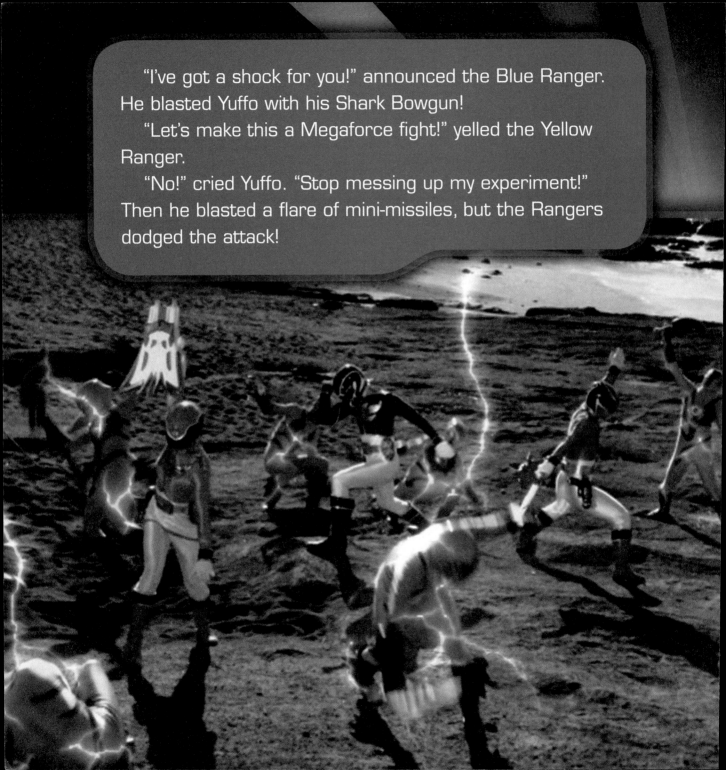

"I've got a shock for you!" announced the Blue Ranger. He blasted Yuffo with his Shark Bowgun!

"Let's make this a Megaforce fight!" yelled the Yellow Ranger.

"No!" cried Yuffo. "Stop messing up my experiment!" Then he blasted a flare of mini-missiles, but the Rangers dodged the attack!

Now it was the Rangers' turn to fight back. The Blue Ranger swiftly tackled Yuffo and blasted the alien with his Shark Bowgun. Yuffo crashed down in a dazed heap.

"Let's try an experiment of our own!" said the Blue Ranger. "The Megaforce Blaster!"

"Right!" said the rest of the Rangers.

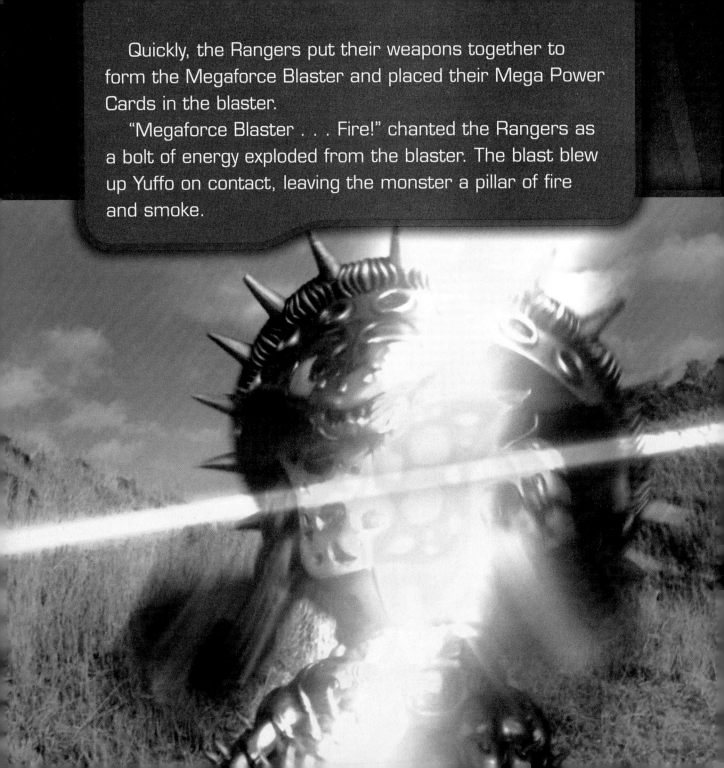

Quickly, the Rangers put their weapons together to form the Megaforce Blaster and placed their Mega Power Cards in the blaster.

"Megaforce Blaster . . . Fire!" chanted the Rangers as a bolt of energy exploded from the blaster. The blast blew up Yuffo on contact, leaving the monster a pillar of fire and smoke.

Watching from the Warship deck, Admiral Malkor, Vrak, and Creepox were enraged.

"Vrak!" Admiral Malkor shouted viciously. "Unleash your pets!"

The sound of beating wings filled the room as a flock of batlike creatures swarmed around Vrak. "My royal weapon. I'll send my Zombats down at once!"

And the swarm of Zombats darted toward planet Earth.

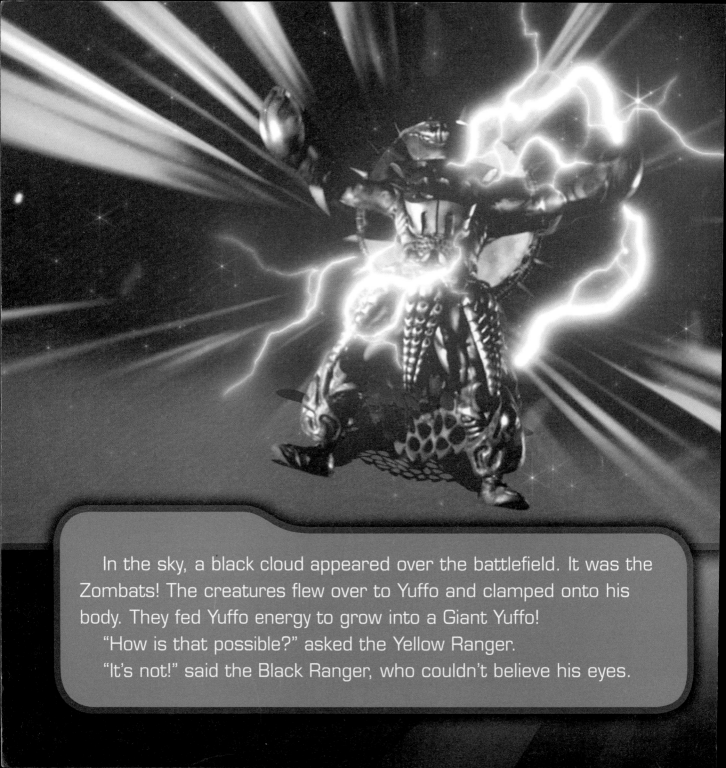

In the sky, a black cloud appeared over the battlefield. It was the Zombats! The creatures flew over to Yuffo and clamped onto his body. They fed Yuffo energy to grow into a Giant Yuffo!

"How is that possible?" asked the Yellow Ranger.

"It's not!" said the Black Ranger, who couldn't believe his eyes.

But Giant Yuffo was very real . . . and very dangerous. As the beast blazed the Rangers with massive fiery explosions, Gosei contacted them from afar. "Rangers! There are even greater powers at your command. Take these Power Cards and use them wisely!"

The Rangers pulled out cards with images of their Zords!

Then the Rangers called forth their Zords, which were hidden on a distant, deserted island. These ancient Zords were ready for battle. They blasted off the island and zipped through the air to fight alongside the Rangers.

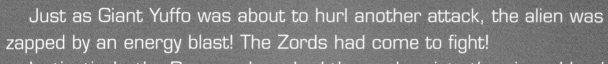

Just as Giant Yuffo was about to hurl another attack, the alien was zapped by an energy blast! The Zords had come to fight!

Instinctively, the Rangers launched themselves into the air and landed in their Zords' cockpits.

Angered by the Zords, Giant Yuffo split into a dozen flying saucers and raced after them.

The flying saucers pumped out clouds of thick black smoke. The Red Ranger couldn't see a thing! Luckily, the Dragon Mechazord managed to dive out of the smoke.

The Phoenix Mechazord soared through a highway tunnel to outrun a set of flying saucers. They almost caught the Pink Ranger when the Red Ranger blasted them!

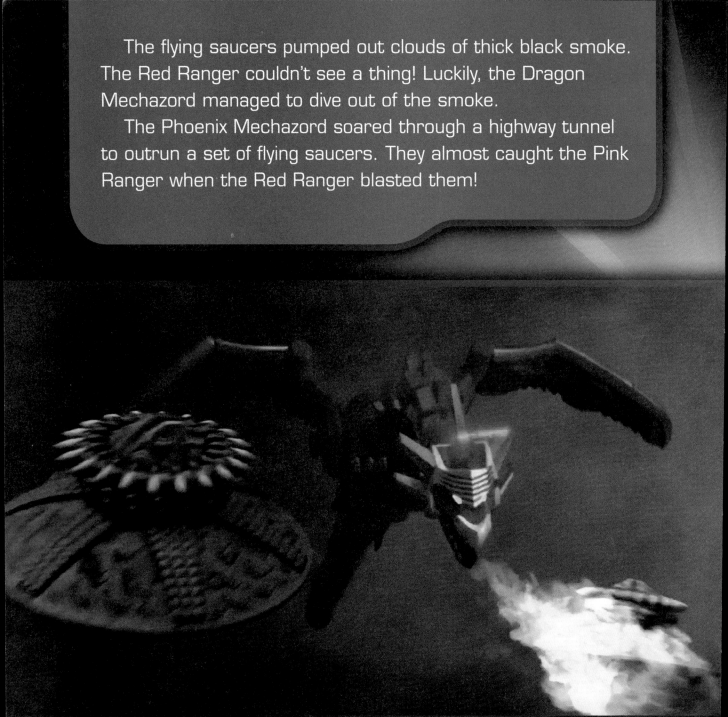

The Shark Mechazord tracked two more flying saucers underwater and blasted them with torpedoes!

On land, the Snake Mechazord wrapped around four flying saucers. One of them escaped, but it didn't get far. The Tiger Mechazord chomped it and hurled it to the ground, where the alien saucer exploded.

The last flying saucer transformed back into Giant Yuffo. "Impressive, but ultimately useless!" he declared.

But Gosei had another idea. To defeat the monster, the Rangers could combine their Zords to create the Megazord!

All of the Zords snapped into place like huge puzzle pieces to form the Megazord and the Rangers were teleported to the five-station cockpit.

Giant Yuffo struck first with a blistering fireball, but the Megazord easily dodged the blast!

Then the Rangers attacked with the MegaPunch and MegaKick. They launched Megazord's arms and legs at Giant Yuffo. The Zords battered the alien with a swarm of rocket-powered kicks and punches!

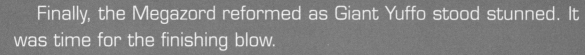

Finally, the Megazord reformed as Giant Yuffo stood stunned. It was time for the finishing blow.

"Victory Charge, activate!" they shouted in unison. "For Planet Earth and all who live on it—attack!"

The Megazord's flaming sword glared with power as it sliced Giant Yuffo with the Great Strike! There was a mega-explosion as Yuffo was defeated once and for all.

Back on the Warstar Ship, Admiral Malkor was furious! He couldn't believe that the Rangers had beaten Giant Yuffo.

"Well, that was a failed experiment!" he yelled. "If we are to conquer this planet we must get rid of those Rangers!"

On Earth, the teens celebrated their victory. Everyone realized that it was bravery and teamwork that had saved the day.

While all the Rangers were awesome on their own, they were unbeatable as a team.